A PAWLEYS ISLAND ANTHOLOGY

a collection of poems

&

other musings

by

Kenneth P. Smith

Middleton House Publishing, Ltd., Co.
Greenville, SC
2024

All characters and places in this book are fictitious and are the results of the author's imagination. Any resemblance to any persons, living or dead, is strictly coincidental.

FIRST EDITION

Pawleys Island Anthology, a collection of poems & other musings

ISBN: 978-0-9981071-9-6

TABLE OF CONTENTS

THE ISLAND

MOVEMENT IN THE SHADOWS

MUSINGS

To Mary

Works by Kenneth P. Smith

- None But The Living (novel; 2017)
- Bad Creek (novel; 2020)
- Mill Town (novel; 2022)
- Pawleys Island Anthology (poetry: 2024)

Author's Notes

No cliché is more accurately applicable to the arts than, 'beauty is in the eye of the beholder'. It speaks to, I think, the subjectivity of the arts, all the arts. And I believe that of all the arts, none is more subjective than poetry. Subjective to some degree to the poet, but more so to the reader. Subjective to the extent that readers say, 'this speaks to me' or 'this is rubbish' or 'this poem is beautiful' or 'I don't understand it.' All these comments might be expressed from different people reading the same poem.

To me, poetry–better poetry, anyway–is emotional. That is, it is emotions expressed in language. But it is emotions passed through the prism of experience. The emotions are specific to the poet as well as to the reader, and they are likely seldom identical. Sometimes not even close.

The poems and writings in this collection were writing over several decades. I started writing them as a young man and stopped writing them as an older one when I turned to writing novels. I felt that I had expressed myself as much in poetry as the gods would permit. So, I have compiled and published them to share with you in this anthology.

Although I was born and reared in the upstate of South Carolina, the low country and particularly the sea have become a part of my life to which I have a strong attachment and affinity. I first visited the South Carolina coast with my family at age six when we took a vacation to Charleston and to Edisto Island. As a teenager, of course, I frequented Myrtle Beach and Ocean Drive in the summers. Finally, in the early nineteen-seventies I "discovered" Pawleys Island and Litchfield, and my love affair with the Low Country was consummated. I currently have a small place at Pawleys, on the marsh near Litchfield beach.

In *Pawleys Island Anthology* are contained the poems I have written about the sea and this area of South Carolina. They are, to me, emotions filtered through my experiences of the Low Country and life–both good and bad. The other collection, *Movement in the Shadows,* contains a wider range of poems, somewhat more esoteric and experimental, which deal with life and love and how I have viewed or experienced it. Also included in the anthology are several stories and musings–more like sketches, actually–written from personal observations of my world and the people in it.

So, this work is really a love song. A love song of words and emotions, but more accurately a love song with the dark, rich, mysterious Low Country of South Carolina, its people and, of course, the sea.

I don't write poetry now, for as I alluded to earlier, it is a younger man's pursuit. You may have noted that I have dedicated this collection, "To Mary," but I hope to make a connection to anyone who reads it and, thus, will in some way become my friend as well. I hope the reader will find some joy and perhaps a bit of truth in these poems and musings.

THE ISLAND

Marsh Air

Sweet salt breeze wash
me clean.
Wash away the dirt of life
and lift
Me to flying out ever
the sea,
To breathe this vapor of
time gone
Then regained by drifting
lightly over
The tide's strength of sameness,
endless motion.
Wash away my vague traces in
the sand.
Leave it smooth and creaseless
again, stretch
Its vast white ribbons before me,
let me
Live here and die here
not alone
Sweet salt breezes wash
me clean.

Autumn Sea

Emerald sea beat your song
against the wind.
Draw me close and let me
touch your soul.
Let the time we share
lift us both
Above your endless tide.
Emerald sea beat your song.

Beneath Spanish Moss

Old men on the porch to sleep,
Children in the street
Play out their games and
And never wonder how
The two shall ever meet.

Blue Hot Jamaica

blue hot Jamaica
you are what love should be

cast adrift in shimmering
white seas

this pinch of earth
left but to beauty

to await the return
of some timeless suitor

rain down your sweet potion
hold me tenderly

til the warm moment
when you let me go

cool green Jamaica
you are what love should be

The Buoy

Out off the point, beyond the rocks
Is a beacon telling ships where to lay
And guiding them home.
On cold winter nights I walk the shore there and
See it blinking far out in the dark water.
How lonely the sentinel is,
Bearing the burden of life.
I turn, collar up, shivering,
I see the floating light
Far out.
Glancing back, I head for home.

Flying

From the back porch of the cottage you could see
The dunes with their tall grass and the sea
Stretching out, endlessly it seemed,
To touch the sky and glisten in the sun.
I used to think it such fun
And a good way to pass the time
To watch ships passing by with their tall white sails,
Like eagle's wings spread, in rhyme
With the gently rolling swells.
It was easy then to dream and see
Of far-off places where ships go
And return home only for a time
And then, with the sea calling, be gone again
To dark and sometimes magic places, or at least they seemed so
Because they were so different from the things I knew.
But I only sat and watched them pass by
And I wished that I
Were up high in the mast
Clinging to it, almost flying in the wind.
From there I could look to where I was going
And back to places I have been.
But from the porch of the cottage the summers slipped by
Almost unnoticed until I
Realized one day that I too could fly
Before the wind and skim the shiny blue wake
Just as I had dreamed of doing many times before.
And I do that now, sail I mean.
And I have often seen,
When my ship comes close to shore,
Boys looking back at me and
I wave to them but never beckon.
For they must choose if they will be
A watcher of ships passing by.

Night Sea

The stellar board has shrouded
the straight horizon
And cast her diamonds out
        to play,
Children bright and moving
Across the universe's silent yard.

You cannot learn to love here,
this harbor of the night.
        The cold gray light of dawn
Will shred you to pieces and
Leave your shallow thoughts
        upon the sand.

Your soul must be
born here,
        Brought forth before the night
Pushed fears and passion aside,
Your body only follows you
        To be content with the sea
To love its night,
To dance to its ghostly song.

Sand Traces

In a chilling misty dawn
Lay traces in the sand,
Lines before the battle drawn
Across a dormant land.

Sketched there on the frozen beach
Their winding trail soon ran
Just within the water's reach
And lost their touch with land.

Sand

Shining, sparking in the sun
It's not aimed at anyone.
It's gone as quick as its begun,
The coolness seldom lingers.

Diamonds in the breaking light,
Leaving shadows of the night,
Briefly before the morning's flight,
And the sun's outstretched fingers.

Walking there, beneath my feet,
Wet and gleaming crystals meet,
Fleeting still before the heat
In colors not of sorrow.

And in the evening I'm glad to learn
Just before the night's return
That all before me begins to yearn
And lives until tomorrow.

Sea Wind

Winds that lift the birds,
        chill the human heart.
They drown the useless words and
        Tear our dreams apart.

Southern Nights

I have walked in honeysuckled dreams
On warm southern nights
Steaming, lost.
With things hot and near.
But daring not to touch,
Or see them
Too closely for fear they would vanish
In the blistering dawn.
In days gone
Before me and melancholy hours
I have spent lingering over things and
Vapors long past
Its empty desires and hot-blooded passions,
Only to wake briefly to hear the torture
Of wasted youth
Burning in my soul.
But the trick of time,
Restless above
Our pitiful shouts, is in looking back,
How sweet the world was,
How soft the wind,
How bright the sun.

Spanish Bayonets

Growing thick and deadly,
Dew hides the emerald edge,
Was ever a man so desperate
Who leaped and grasped the ledge?

Summer

Summer is a quick chance
        to be that young again
Pasted on the windless days
        burnt-laughing
In wasted ways of freedom
Swimming in glimmering
        hazy mirages
Find that (lost) love
        gone
Lost innocence
        Not worth keeping
and return the
        child they knew
You could be

Sun Days

The flashing rock, hard and white
Grinds beneath its edge
The legends of lost warriors,
Vicious and proud,
Who saw the land as air
And could not understand the beads,
Only survival.
White water, frothy with ancient and
False purity
Washes over the brown stain
Filling up the footprints left there
Then evaporating into a silvery mist,
To be blown away by a million
Screaming breezes.
The small brown girl
Hunched digging in the sand
Looked up at me
With smiling eyes.

The Creek

The murky creek winds lazily through
The wet golden marsh and to
The sea whose child it is.
Relying on the dependable tide to
Fill it again when it empties its wash.
Crabs, and there are some shrimp where it washes back,
Run and scatter in the black
Mud on the bottom as the water
Returns to the ocean and is, to be sure,
A part of it.

I have spent long hours, indeed
My boyhood, it seems on the creek fishing
And riding its energy
Away from a world which did not
Seem quite so friendly or a part of me.

In early days it had been a road
With barges loaded with heavy bales
Causing the boats to ride low in the water.
And friends would come down too,
And out across the marsh you
Could see them waving, and run
Down to the dock and know

That the night would be festive.
The creek has never changed
And I don't think it will, but strange
How I think of it when thinking back.

The Death of Annie Jenkins

She always came at evening, to the church,
When it was cooler and seemed quieter
Although it was still in the churchyard.
Peaceful it was there, more like a large dark ballroom
Beneath the moss-laden trees.
Thin lines of light pierced through its roof
As the sun lay westward, it would soon be gone.
These candles flickered in the faint breeze
And caused the grass to change hue beneath her feet.
She always came alone, with the handful of flowers,
To lay them gently on her mother's grave.
She seldom lingered in this familiar place
But merely did what she had come to do.
There were other things that were to be attended to
Now that she was the lady of the house
Or so her father sometimes teased.

Only the sexton was there and
She always nodded to him shyly and he to her.
But his day was made and ended with her arrival
And he always waited there beside the church door,
Watching her walk down the dusty road, gracefully he thought.
How lovely she was, young and fragile,
A wispy beauty, of blood, and much like
The stars to him, or gold, beyond reach.
He always meant to speak to her,
Perhaps ask about her family or the planting.
But he never did or could.
So he merely smiled and nodded each day as she passed
On her way to the family plot.

He waited by the old church door this day
Pondering if she would come.
The northeast sky was beginning to roar and boil
And the wind pushed hard against the old oaks,
Bending them a little and causing their mossy beards to sway,
Casting eerie, dancing shadows on the earth below.

The storm would come with darkness
From the ocean a mile away.
And the melancholy churchyard and its keeper
Waited for her in silence, dreading the night ahead.
He walked out to the old tree, black and gnarled,
Beside the grave.
Here he could see her, almost touch her,
But she would never know.

She did come that day, late in the afternoon.
But hurried she was for the storm was moving in
And she was a little frightened.
He held his breath and wept quietly as
She knelt beside the grave and placed the flowers there.
It was then that the old man reached out;
Old craggy fingers with a death grip
Around the young frail throat.
She struggled only slightly, for it was not in her spirit,
And fell limp and lifeless across her mother's grave.

Winter Geese

The geese of winter whose magic flight
Soared ‘cross frozen waste
To see above the exploding dawn,
Where circled clear and high
The leaders of the sky on
A maiden voyage home.

The geese of winter, those metallic birds
Of speed and natural grace,
Were given a gold spun song
Of shouted music without words,
Awkward notes of melodies soon
Forgotten ‘neath echoes of darkened rooms.

The geese of winter, vagrants of the sky,
Have shirked a narrowed passage
Between arrow lifted flight and
A labor where ancient beauty sighs
The breath of reaching up to take
A softer kiss than man could ever make.

The Tabby Makers*

Coming down to the ribbon beach early
Together and singing not too sadly
But soft enough to sooth
The creatures lying there
And loud enough to wake man.
Black and strong
They are bound by useless labor.
Gathering the pink and blue shells,
Crusty and gritty,
From the sand;
Homes left eons ago by tiny monsters
Devouring themselves,
Until the coarse brown bags are
Bulging and full.
They lose some when hoisting them up
But most are safe.
The foreman, lord of lords,
Shouts to them
For they have only done this
Forever and
Mixing in the salty brew
They, or some master, can build.
Build his home, a stable, a walk.
Or a wall
A cell
A tomb.

*Tabby, an African word, is a type of concrete made by burning oyster shells to create lime, then mixing it with water, sand, ash and broken oyster shells. Tabby was used by early Spanish settlers in present-day Florida, then by British colonists primarily in coastal South Carolina and Georgia.

Child

very tiny child
what will you leave me
you are only earthly briefly
to dance upon this land
in beauty and innocence

When

When the winds blow cold and there's froth upon the waves,
    I won't forget to put red roses on your grave.
When I've loved you long and know that's all I gave,
    I won't forget to put red roses on your grave.
When memories of you are all I have to save,
    I won't forget to put red roses on your grave.
When in still and lonely times I am not so brave,
    I won't forget to put red roses on your grave.
When I recall our youthful time and all to us it gave,
    I won't forget to put red roses on your grave.
When you an angel bending near the earth survey,
    I'd like to think you'll put red roses on my grave.

Sea Wind

I am the wind.
Who can stand before me
and
Not be changed by my fragrant presence?
Who has not been hammered by my strength?
Who has not been gently and erotically
Caressed by my soft fingers?
You who face me and look into my eyes
Are soon disarmed.
I have blown dust ever the bones
of greater men than you.
I have swept away your gnarled past and
Left it smooth as glass.
The grass that worked to cover your blood
so well
I have bent down in passing.
Across your finite plains I have lent my power
briefly, then snatched it away.
I am the wind.
Who can deal with me?

Winter Sea

The silent blue mist wraps itself
Around the weathered cottages,
The thin ribbon of beach before me
Glows in the wet moonlight
Until it vanishes in the cold shroud.
The roaring hammers of waves
Beat their constant rhythm,
The night is new here and the air young.
Here I rendezvous with my first love,
Here I settle with all around me in peace,
Here I meet with the sea.

An Old Man Walking Away

It was the last day I was on the beach,
The sun hung motionless, hot and fiery.
The sand stretched out before me,
Shimmering and melting in the hot wet air.
I could see just beyond the point, in the haze,
The old man walking away from me.
Walking in the ocean's edge to keep
The sand from scorching his feet.
I had seen him here before
But not that far down the beach.
I watched him as he became a tiny black moving speck
And then disappeared into the sweltering haze.

MOVEMENT IN THE SHADOWS

A Feather Breath of Life

a feather breath of life
moves like a mist
slowly where the tropic waters
meet and mingle in
the warmth only moving gently
to push the moment on
in this garden tunnel where love seeps
out in giving what is there
and sleeps the sleep that comes
when two are one again

A thousand days later

a thousand days later
the one of them
caught my i
briefly not time to count
only played
the joke was on me
as it usually is
during
vodka with
a twist
the night away
holding bygone lies
at bay
and enjoying
the mad rhapsody
that was me with
my clown sad truth
that no one bought
only pressed
their noses against
the cold
window and
stared glassily

A Wherever Life

lying slowly in the darkness
with a gentler domain of wet sounds
resting troubled soul
        a passion quieted
        a peace subdued

of door closed moments in endless
rhythms beating sounds above the
vacuumed noise the tender rain
        hold me gently as i go
        let me sound the leaving

the bursting forth of golden life
on twice played stages sets the moment
in elegant etched time with burning splendor
        with god's fingered song
        and children angel free

do not leave here quietly
or saintly go where wisdom leads
we must we will wage a golden war
        with a whatever moment
        a wherever life

All tangled up in hurt

all tangled up in hurt
we see ourselves
only
darkly moving
against the silent storm
the star kissed lover
gone quietly
out the door
a day in
the sun
from foolish life
to a
wisdom filled
death
and maybe never
seeing the
silent love
of one behind
who is us

your hammered heart was your hurt

your hammered heart was your hurt
and your honor
lifting painfully above the rush
of gateless time
endlessly seeking a stepped rhythm
as hard spring flowers fought the tide
a tumultuous and whispered peace
was said before grace and
without grace the dead movement came
the friendly moment was briefest hope
when cocooned love shattered light
scattered grief as daisy petals do
beneath the wicked feet of a
sordid crowd bent on coming homeward
it's not this peak of crystal vision that
catches you looking seaward
it must be the air salt that
pricks the teared eye

And Josie Was Drunk That Day

and josie was drunk that day
        as the day before,
she sat sun struck in the
        white hot shade
and huge black flies stung
        on her legs and
other places

she sweated and smelled
        and swore at the shrapnel junk
he sold for laughs,
        she'd had enough she'd leave
watching him breath and snore
        she didnt need this
She told herself

Blessed

How is it that we, blest beyond belief and comprehension,
Would choose the baser depths of our inclinations,
And with passion for disembodied loneliness
Embrace the lesser angels of our nature,

When we, with false compassion, seek a world
Foretold, not realizing that the existence
We now would have in ever-fleeting time
Is but a breath or perhaps only a touch away?

With blameless humanness we are transcribed
To be trapped eternally in an endless maze of trying
To reach with grasping hands
What we already possess in our soul and heart,

Only, as the sweet and winged dove of our own salvation,
Is to be set free and but returns to us from the descending flood
With the green fresh branch of our own future and hope,
That is, to say, ourselves.

Caught in the Dispersion

Caught in the dispersion of foreign stares
In mourning the death of a Jew I did not know,
Like pallid ghost in the morning drizzle
The store fronts line my morning walk
Seeing him among them, one of them really,
And his pride, the sacrifice made before
A god of anonymity.

What wrest the fellow from
His unreal dreams seen by dark-eyed children
that melt angel's faces,
He they matched against an innocence
That never was?
Am I losing his face in the ghastly crowd
In death-bent suffering I could never know?

The perfect peace was said long ago
And cast this tribe man to be eons of
Himself as cauldron hatreds over the dreaded earth
Shredded his skin and heart,
Twelve perfect rivers flowed blue cleared to blackness
But only a shared whisper made them one.

The holocaust of perjured goodness
Cost me a friend I did not know.

Class of '65

The light breeze flicked up the corner
Of the flag, letting the sunlight
Dance on the slick dark mahogany.
At least that's one way to get home
I thought, when none of us felt like heroes
Or wished him to be one.

As the winds licked the wet spring fields
We just let him go, with him looking on,
I think, fixed on a fading dream.
But being there was our own small virtue
When none was needed, just a little more
Time to learn what summers really means.

Now Norma sits by the window looking out,
Humming softly to herself and weeping as the
Moon goes and cars flashed by in the darkness.

Dark Night Dark Girl

Dark night dark girl
Selling self-belief
For a song
She's tough and knows it
The only way she can
Hard street hard men
Both beneath her feet
But they pay
Money and more
It's all enough
God not rain again
Wet night wet self
In more ways than one

Footprints Gently Tripping

footprints gently tripping
over scattered reams of time
voices in the shadows
i stop to see if they're mine

the past in frozen stillness
melts within my hand
runs through my trembling fingers
to haunt my dreams again

the visions of her beauty
cast in yellow light
are my glory in believing
and my hell each tortured night

the bitterness of never loving
that was meant to be
being all the different lovers
but always me always me

haggle with the spent

haggle with the spent
                    virtues
strike a better deal
get a bargain if
                    you can
only i live with me
to make a shaky
                    peace

Hail Full Moon

Hail full-moon
    Silver dollar
You slipped up there
    quickly
This cold October night:
    Farmer's light
Ghost's delight.
    Magic on her front doorsteps
That young year
    She's forgotten.
We loved love
    Brushing kisses away
As if they were
    Free forever.

he went crazy on

he went crazy on
        some ink-nights

losing his voice in silence
        ending in forced solitude

gold spun dreams
        of smiles and love

the heavy ooze of
        past thickness

cloud air future presently is
        one himself

pained to unforgiving

Her

Her
Perfume, the perfume
made
me crazy
now and then
(and fragrant as
youth days
spilled)
And she was
as fate would
have it
beautiful
Wouldn't you know
it
I couldn't have
Her
but quick fantastic
days were ours
through
a wall as thin
as paper

Hey Little Boy

hey little boy
me but for
forty years

come dancing
this way
audacity to burn
sun energy

who loves a
crystal rain
joys a day
believing you can

you bursting with
light and
life

how can I but
cry and sing
seeing you
paint my dreams

I Am Better for Having Loved You

I am better for having loved you
And died the sweet death of bitter self,
To be lost and found in the same breath,
To have died upon your breast only
To be born in your arms again.

When soul to soul becomes one,
To be pressed together as a rose
Between the pages of life's weight,
The sweet sighs of those leaves
Comfort me now, as not before.

Never again to rise alone
To shout my own living,
For life alone is death or worse,
But in the shadows or in the sun,
There was you, always you.

Reach not for me now or cling to
The love that gauged its own passing,
But with spring's first soft breeze
Or when autumn's warning chill comes calling,
Think of me with you
When time seemed forever.

i am fooled

i am fooled by
this darting blond
atom
into a perhaps world
believing
earth is a child
or could be
again

in the whatever
moment
when its clear
i am he
he me
my heart becomes my brain

my man the boy
with the power
of turning
things right

I became her man darkly

I became her man darkly
That exploding summer
When air died
Late August
And young as she was.
Traced in wet sand
Was our quarter year
Washed quickly seaward,
I, the soft reality of the past,
Knew had doomed us both
To walking back
Alone.

i bled screams

i bled screams
in your whispered snow
losing my soul
as life
exploded three or four times giving
me peace
between
the blistered
hot canyon walls
into an eye of darkness
turned to light

i can touch

i can touch the
corn silk hair
and hear the tiny heart
endure the steps
of awkward flight
first to know the flashes
of changing worlds
in splendid broken form
i would but
i cant be the one
who smiles and grows and loves

i hate the razor

i hate the razor
edge of love

knowing passion
can push me

into the abyss
on either side

the ecstasy of
a moment quick

wisdom eclipsed
of having it all

lost me
your heart

i have sought the leggy world

i have sought the leggy world
to slip between its passion
for shallow dignity
buried by what it does

light quick glances become
only chances to meet yourself
no the animal across the room
who pumps your blood into hot rhythms

sell yourself but not me
short on some dingy street
melting in a city of humanity
mine now but i'll taste it later

i move uneasy

i love uneasy
        movements across your
        incidental smile
your broken sadness is mine
a little
and for a while
like tarnished coins i shine
        and give back to you
why trust me
with money
        but you do some
let me black hate the sky
for you
and scream at it
        know your magic
thoughts
mother earth has moved
        beneath you
not me this time just you
the gone sorrow
        that is
your pain
you will hold
        and love it
for a time
then me

i

i
saw
you
through
the
smoke
and
smiled
but
your
grace
flight
ended
angel
faced
girl
with
a
tear
exploding
a nervous
quiet
cough
no words

i was born

i was born
in the dead of winter
juxtaposed with greatness
if breathing is

weaned on
gentle ineptness
songs slung across
gentler heaving
breasts

never forgetting
monster fingers
shadows
dancing on the ceiling
chance friends
that were not

only silly faces
made worse
against poignant
thunder
later

ice like

ice like
the stucco wall is
cool and white
rough and smooth
an old man's face
patterns
square and deep
chiseled there
maps of other things
the fan beats the high hot air
girls sweat
men breathe heavy and loud
i drink the bitter water
how i dread the sun

if the Moon

if the moon
sucks its life
from the sun
as they would have
us believe
then perhaps
lovers and wars
being spent
in prostituted light
are fooled
as we thought
all along
into thinking
for them it's
different
but slip past sliding
their own
frail visions
in deluded
brightness

In Time Spun Cocoons

In time-spun cocoons
We peered at each other's
            naked minds
And bodies
In murky silver mirrors.
Swaying shadows,
            wall-waltzing
Battling a suffering dying candle
Was love or
            near to it
As we cared to be.
I chanced to see more,
            Danced to the music
Of fragile grace,
Thread-hung upon your hand
            Finger me away.

Choices

Is three days enough
Or does it take a lifetime?
Or an eternity?

In only an instant,
A difference is made.
Is three days enough
Or does it take a lifetime?
Or an eternity?
In only an instant,
A difference is made.

it's hard to take

it's hard to take
fiberglass seriously
so
pretentious and exact
molded into
perfect form of
what
ever
someone else
thought it should be
not like
at all wood or
leather
whose perfect
imperfection
never
casts doubt
on our humanness
but
feels right
in our
hands

I've counted the hours

I've counted the hours too
Many times to think they
Mean anything

Other than what they are,
Tiny wrung drops of life
That bead up and run

Down the cool side of
A glass of Jack that
Leaves a ring on the table

Beside where I work and
Sometimes sleep, but very
Little of either.

Slumbering Madonnas and restless
Whores are the same when
Your vision is blurred

By the blue smoke of
Pall Malls and of Spain and
What they said it would be like.

But she says she can't be
What your chisel would work
Out of soft, giving marble

Joy to the world

Joy to the world
Bang the bell
Pierce the quietness
Of fire,
But see the fine
Linen laid
Beyond a measured
Note when
All gather quickly
To pronounce
The breaking day,
Crowning the
Ice with gold.

Late

I arrived at the crossroads much later than I had planned,
I had been delayed,
And I knew he wouldn't understand
Or humor me in my indolence or excuses,
But he was there, of course,
With the annoying impatience of someone
Who knows the score,
Someone who knows you better than you know yourself.

There was no questioning,
I hesitated but thanked him just the same,
He sighed and I knew he would not
Judge me nearly as harshness as I
Did myself.

He had been here many times before,
At the crossroads, I knew this and
I admired him and was thankful for his ambivalence.
So many times, so many losses,
But some won.

I pulled my coat collar up around me,
It was not so cold as it was lonely,
It seemed like cold, it felt like cold,
But it was only lonely,
There was no beckoning to the roads,
They all looked pretty much the same.

His sad smile was one of knowing,
one of knowing he had done all he could
Know or do,
He knew better than I that he could do nothing more
But meet me at the crossroads.

And I had been late arriving there,
I had been other places seeking comfort
But knowing

I was prolonging the time and the meeting at the
Crossroads, the meeting with him.

He smiled and we spoke quietly in the twilight,
And sipped from a silver flask
That he pulled from his jacket pocket,
To dull the pain I suspected that we both felt.
He was kind in that way but unrelenting.

I knew without compass he was useless to me
And I suppose me to him.
He touched my shoulder lightly and
We looked into each other's faces.
He said, "I can do no more than meet you here."
I replied, "I know, but it is enough."

For a moment in the light evening breeze
We both gazed at the crossroads,
Then I moved on without his pointing the way,
And he turned and walked back down the lonely road.

Life at 56 (MPH)

I sit on the porch, screened from bugs and life,
Smoking, which I shouldn't be doing,
They tell me,
In the heavy warm dampness of summer twilight.
A few cars go by on the street
But I only half-see the blur of red taillights
As I glance down at my hands,
Recalling my father's,
How old they looked that last day,
With thick blue veins 'neath skin
Thin and delicate as parchment,
Shocked at the revelation, in the back yard
In youthful stupidity,
Never thinking they could be my own hands
Without the honor of labor that his bore.
My pipe goes out as I smack the burnt
Taste against my lips.
Knocking out the ashes into the small clay vase,
I go inside where it is cooler.

Like/Don't Like

I like soup if it's not too hot
And chocolate milk when its not

I don't like haircuts, never will
The barber makes me sit so still

I like the beach at the shore
I only wish I could go there more

I don't like spinach, a slimy thing
If I eat too much, I might turn green

I like birds, I don't know why
But I bet I would if I could fly

I don't like the dark that comes with night
So by my bed there's a little light

I like the moon whose face I see
It makes me laugh when he smiles at me

I like dogs who nuzzle me
I wish I knew what they think they see

I don't like books that end too soon
But I'm afraid this one's done.

Missionary

The pain
Thin and gray
Is always with me

As I pass
From emerald day to
Emerald day.

I stoop to touch
The half-white child
Who
Does not yet yearn
For our porcelain
World.

Touching her
I move on
Beneath a blasting
Sun
That warms the dirt street
And
Burns the deep sky
To the fire beyond.

on baked white walls

on baked
white walls too
hard
to see
with unshielded eyes
closed
we writhe
in pagan dance
until
we drop
as shadows will
at
evenings cool
and singularly bound
to
a future
beyond our bullet sweat

On bow-bent boughs where archers played

On bow-bent boughs where archers played
Their thin high songs which seem to lay
Out beyond where birches linger.

A dog-eared page of time has seen
And marked its place, from silence gleaned
A small sad voice turned to anger.

To jump to the icy brooks to fly
Without air to breathe yet not to die
Like a beating bird ground to danger.

The war dead are healthier though
Than those freaks of life just below
The frost line of her single finger.

In endless lines the seabirds flew
Beneath a patterned sky and windless knew
They are of the ageless angels.

On snow-covered fields

On snow-covered fields a farmer's dream runs
True like a row of green summer corn;
His heart beat quickly at the heart of spring.

On snow-covered fields a young girl dreams
Of love 'midst caressing breezes and
Time held still by her lover's heart.

On snow-covered fields a general's ambition burns
Away the crusty ice, baring the hard ground
Where he can stand at battle's edge.

On snow-covered fields a young man's life
Ebbs from his soul in scarlet patches,
Hopes torn to pieces, gone his shattered youth.

On thin blue paper

On thin blue
paper lay the world
a 6 x 6 square
of reason

I could point here
or there to this place that
It somehow was reasonable
to suppose this was
what (where) we were

Til the big smelly
guy punched
his cigar out
black on Africa

Passage

We came in quiet succession
Laughing on the inside
Bleeding outwardly,
Touching red and brown earth
Cool and hot
Under the stare of the full-grown child;
Seeing and not knowing
The dirty, shifting cities that
Surround him.
And cursing his breath and
The heavy air.
Then leaving under a warm rain of rusting iron
With nostrils flared in an acrid wind,
And fire
At our fingertips
To soothe the melted minds.

Perspectives

It is not with endless pleasure
Or timeless sweet delight
Nor do I return with laughter
To those painful searing flights
Which some men hold as treasure and
still others live their dreams
In days gone forever midst scenes
Of broken time.
It is not with sorrow pining
Or glistening tears of joy
That I recall a time long spent
When I was keen on grasping
The world's sweet juice and
Drinking it down lustily
With friends and lovers too.
It is not with conquering glory
Or knowledge that I lived
In a time past, whose story
Is unfolding
As it dashes, leaps along.
It is as though I have slept and dreamed
Of moving silently through the dawning
Mist,
Then waking seeing more clearly
The trail left behind in shallow water.
But neither is it with regret
Nor do I count it lest
These times, gone now, when it all seemed
Very real and yet

As I stand upon this hill
I can see three worlds, behind me and beyond.
But the thing that I can feel and touch,
Is real and very good,
It is all that matters,
It is now.

Question

If I came to die here
For reasons only known to me,
If the time was but the season
For life to set me free,
And if our time together
Was no more than before
When we thought we had forever
And wished no minute more,
Could you understand the difference
And love me just the same,
If you knew the tide was turning
And the sea called out my name,
If you knew nights would be this lonely
And the wind could be so cold,
Could you think of me so warmly
As you did when I was home?
I have no fear in dying
Less the pain in life I've known,
But the sadness that haunts my spirit
Is in leaving you all alone.

she's tall she's cool

she's tall she's cool
she's no one's fool
but herself
almost strangled
in a perhaps passion
of young dreams
so much beauty
a pretty face
an elegant lie
stone blue eyes
cry a sigh
as forty is a death

Silent Boy

silent boy
run quickly
into the golden
eye of dreams
save your sighs
for later
when youll
need them
wake
you laughing
child
play in
the rain
soaked wind
give me
a smile
of time and
be gone

Spring and Winter

spring and winter
locked horns
today
in a desperate windy fight
spring
who would be gentler
aroused
like a napping cat
with a certain
natural fierceness
would not be quieted
and older winter
was determined
too
with hard gray lines
these
held and gnarled actors
from an ancient script
played out
to the death each time
til both with
tired aching arms
drew back
but spring
with soft even
breath
becomes
the
victor

spring is no friend of mine

spring is no friend of mine
or of yours
if youve lived much
or loved violently at least once
with its lush green wetness
in witness of familiar and longed for passion
exploding colors of light and sound
but with a soft dullness
that smoothes the travelled spirit
it covers quickly the reality of winter
when with cleared eyed bleakness
you could see the day around you
it warms the vivid frigid mind
in drowsy easy touches
teases and caresses
i long for what it cannot bring
new again as it pretends

sprinkled gold

sprinkled gold
    across your face

with dark
    smart
        shining eyes

touch me
    softly quickly
        leave me

take this symmetry

take this symmetry
from me
this soldier straight
                guide
who stands at my door
on pervasive black nights
let my soul
            unravel
                    on your
                            floor
to lie there unpatterned
with ends frayed
unfused and still
ready to begin
again

the artful usurper

the artful usurper
nicked
in the just
of time
a new
frame
from the frigid
stagnant cold
lending
a moment of
subtle greatness
to live eyes
a
somehow push
to be youth
mad again
beneath
a blue diamond sky
turn
in the infant sun
your child
heart
beating winter
carpets
in silver
rain

the bullet rains of april

the bullet rains of april
foolish men young again
see themselves as boy kings
as power magic
drifts across warm dreams
of sleeping in the grass
on sunny afternoons
before the clouds bang

the certain symmetry

the certain symmetry
of some forgotten
may
out beyond the savage wasteland
lie
patterned and smooth
beyond
the mind quick choices
made by a
boy
soldier
who would
a man be
given the time to grow
and never thinking
he wouldn't

the ends of innocence

the ends of innocence
have left me
ragged and undone
my bright path
has been clouded by the sun

subdued
im bent
earthly
youth has helped
slipped in passing
my turn

the tender hope
of loving
turned against me
mist ridden
moon laid
knowledge has left me
weeping

the eye of your rhinestone beauty

the eye of your
        rhinestone beauty
shines sun
        brightly
with love not
        of diamonds
but gleaming
        reflections
in glass mirrors
        washed silver
warm cool
        happy
but unbelieving
        still
with naked
        feeling

The heavy snows of lost Decembers when

The heavy snows of lost Decembers when
Winter's howling message laid
Real upon the heavy carpet,
'Neath bending birches just beyond.

And down the bent traveler then,
Struggling, against the wind
With piercing eyes and icy stares
Just beyond a faint light across the snow.

The light, a yellow light like burnt gold
Has guided the green-head home
Or left his grave to be another place
Where he's found and left to grow.

Out across this endless darkness
Lies moments of flickering life
Spent in peaceful stillness that belies
The coming home of evening's glow.

the not quite

the not quite
spring of loving
you has not left me
breathless as i
had child like
supposed
but dizzy mornings
are sung to places
i slip and slide into
yours
are feelings that
wrap around me
before sweaty thoughtless
laughter

the other room

the other room
you fool
shes down the hall
waiting
in a heavy stillness
smiling coarsely
at
my forced
ineptness
no
truer fool
ever lunged into
a wetter madness knowing
the time and pleasure there
didn't count
at all

the reflected silence

the reflected silence
of the café window
sees me
lost in a mirrored world
only i smile
a little
at the dusk wind
in the park
across the street
truer to me
than i am
cool pictures of now
again
im a smiler
deeply and quickly
as the waiter
serves the coffee

The Dream

I woke to the scream of my own name,
A silent scream to be sure
But a scream just the same,
In the fearful darkness I clutched myself
To know if I was there,
I was not, just an empty cavity
Of sorry nothingness, me,
The source of my own-felt depravity
In the still and heavy night
To be endured moment by moment, waiting
For the hopeless day to come back 'round,
My only hope, in darkness, fading,
The morning broke dull and gray
Without sun
And the tarnished silver sky
Pressed down on me and
The scream was gone but
There was no light,
No light at all.

the hammered quickness

the silver quickness
of your
flagrant smile
wet as rain
sudden thunder
shudders this
tiny bird
dancer
knock again
if you need to
but
me i hammer home

the somehow

the somehow
softness of
your
steps
on dawn
lit floors
awakens wars
and
silly
dreams
wet
sighs
across cool
sheets
frenzied
stillness to
bring
you back

the time spent in crying

the time spent in crying
wasted on
naked shadows
wont or shouldnt
be me
who floated through
youth
and cursed growing
but did
and
liked the smell

the swan song of

the swan song of
the leaf
falling
in lazy flight
to the forest
floor
thundered
through the autumn
hushed
stillness as i
saw my breath
and crunched
them
beneath my feet

the sweet bird movement

the sweet
bird
movement
caught
me praying
her
glancing
across sacred
air
seeing
my sin
of
knowing
too much
what
beauty can
do
but its
only silence
between this
and
a boy
i
remember too
well

there is a certain

there is a certain
violence to this land
that lends (or bends) itself

to pagan songs
sung by godfearing
men

whose timbered
voices seek
muddy truths

eyes that hear
silence
where screams
should be

There is nothing new under the sun

There is nothing new under the sun,
No life destroyed or worlds begun,
Still to see the atom fly
On its eternal senseless road
To being what it can only be,
Or what we think its spinning tells.

Upon this worn and timeless ground
Above the working and the sound
Of soft creation moving toward
Its own sad grave there is
Stale air of others' tombs
Made fresh again before the dawn.

We revolve around the dream
Of time not being what it seems,
As sun and moon follow suit
And pursue the tortured trek
Laid out beyond cries and fears
Of becoming less than we were meant to be.

Thick red wine

Thick red wine
Spilled as blood

Quick drops
On the bar

But Slim the
Bouncer was on me

Without knowing
Why I did the girl

The way I see it
She was on me

As slick as ice
My way wrong

But warm legs
Are worth the trouble

this burnt eyed wisp of a girl

this burnt eyed wisp of a girl
has danced a song of freedom
across my door

where i could see the life
of a thousand dreams
quickly caught in a smile

touch the child but dont
hold her as remembering becomes
a quick glance away

tiny rain dancers

tiny rain dancers
        on plains of late pretending
turn and sparkle
with a million diamonds exploding
        clear bright
just beneath the thin music
an ice blue parody
        of remembering
when in you
believing was seeing

tumbling thoughts are

tumbling thoughts are mine
made
on dizzy afternoons
of
wild jugglers and clowns
screeching smells along
the midway
wilder colors are made
to look real
in
the mustard light
of a
balloons moons
face
on the enchanted
string of laughter
to cool
the silly dreams of fun
come
children we must go
now
its time for supper

we hung out our clothes

we hung out our clothes
	on ma's line in the back yard

dingy laundry hanging
	like madness in the breeze

for all the world to see
	colors run and bleed

in an array of rainbow bleakness
	til we pick them like apples

rags to riches stories
	told twice on stoops in summer

wet words dripped

wet words dripped
into the open tenderness
further than she
was to go
this itching wound
mine to need
filled with me
or some hard sound
of my approach
the black tangled jungle
where all hope was gone
of returning alive
but leaving
them there
swimming and dying
in warm pools
beneath the alabaster
mountain
in black snow

what is love

what is love
but anger and virtues dropped
in hopes of
regaining courage
until at last
its yours
that which seemed unconquerable

or else someone's
dreams of slick wet passion
that you can never know

but hope you can be
magic chances
on golden nights

whatiwantisa

whatiwantisa
june bug summer
blast furnace
air a
blanket of
oppression
stillness where
nothing wants
to move or
can
august melts away
july
and we're
burnt by
waves of white
haze

When It's Only You

T'is madness to think the world's insane
When it's only you that thinks it's flat,
When it's only you that sees the faces and
Hears the voices that aren't there.

The world's not mad nor out of control,
But just spinning like a gyro
That won't be deterred from its course
Once set in timeless motion.

You flay against a burning wind
That lifts birds and planes to flight,
What makes you think that you know differently
When reason says they're right?

why

why
finger me
to
face smooth
dawns
from twisted
nights
when your
beautiful
breathing
exploded over
my loose-gripped
sanity
or was
it
me alone
again
with
rustling
curtains in
a
whispered breeze

Will

I have tried and I have failed.
But having done so
I have seen beyond the horizon.
For her to seek, or for her to try
To overcome her demons,
Or limitations, or problems, or own afflictions,
Must come from within herself;
Drawing upon her own reservoirs of
Strength, courage, faith, or will to win, or
Just to survive.
It cannot be from the will of others or
What someone else desires for her,
Whether out of love, selfish desire, or
Of the purest altruism.
It is, in the end, a matter of choices:
To wallow in the pain and disability of
One's self-consumed universe,
Or to fight its paralyzing grip on
Your body and soul.
Overcoming is a personal thing,
I think,
A walk through one's own shadow
Of the valley of death.
It can't be willed, it can't be wished for.
It simple must be done.
Or not.

wisp of grace

wisp of grace
this lady
has left me
seeing high visions
through
silver dew
sharp light prisms
cut the
patterned arch
of her
long neglected beauty

with breeze songs tripping

with breeze songs tripping
across scented fields
sweet
ripe with pregnant beauty
the year has turned
itself inside out
and has glad given
me you
to
a looking glass to
see
the art of spring

you me

you me
in a circus
with three square rings
working words
performing
dark tricks in even darker mirrors
you always
on the high wire
me in the stands
or
the out back
with the bearded lady
a madness to face
a form that would only
function if we played it right
always right the morning after
over coffee
screaming silence awakened the absurd
loneliness
and fingers sometimes melt together
i did
you did
in a year of moments
our sometime hearts
with the easiness
of old friends laughing at others
who think we dont see
ourselves when
it happened just before the third act
we did me you

you quiver

you quiver
bird-like
in that
brief spelled
moment of
melting
fooling me
believing
primitive powers
are touched
but love
is all
no secret
there

your breath is

your breath is
heavier than your heart

which leads me
to think i imagined

a rain smile
of a girl

with daisy eyes
closer than a touch

who in a penny whisper
tricked me into believing

your whispered touch

your whispered touch
makes spring

come early to me
waiting in the lilac air

above a storm but
in it too

with a peaceful turbulence
just below the

surface of your
smile on me it

rest in the irksome
vividness of living

on you quick life
only love kills

Sonnet

It seems like years since
those days
Of carefree thought and careless ways.
We two, like children, anxious but
sure,
Viewed the world and sought
to lure
Feelings and fun from its tightening
grasp,
To know one another, to feel at last
The bond of something that youth
creates,
Not scared of time, be not late.
I felt to you, and you to me,
We wanted something the other to
see.
But then one day it came to me
That something different was to be.
From that moment, clear and true,
Inside I felt a part of you.
Now the light years and times
are gone,
Stillness lies where winds
have blown.
Those soft spring days and carefree life
Are gone forever, but strife
And storms are also a part
Of this thing which guides
the heart.
Tho' it's not always clear in
What I say and do,
Amidst it all, I still love you.

when the soul of time has vanished

when the soul of time has vanished
like hot breath
breathed in frigid air
and eternity stretches out before you
like space itself
you will find me there
beside you
spirits bound and wound in love
and years

some desperate times of struggle
pain and pleasure
the hand of life has wrought
its finely chiseled face
before us
to remind us
the dying was easy
the living was harder

to believe is the greatest thing
when loves faintly glowing ember
is fanned by a foul wind
form this crazy sorrow
somehow is rendered
a man a woman
who know of the good in each
and in themselves
to be blessed by a gentler
fate

diamonds to be sure
knotted this destined love
beyond asking and dreams
were it not for
war and rain
we would be less
but with you i am more
than i could ever be
alone

This woman who is the earth

This woman, who is the earth,
Has nurtured the unfed soul that is mine.
With strength within her and about her
Majestic unfettered spirit,
Took the seed of my half life
Into the fraction of her own,
And in the sun-warmed field
Brought forth mystery and ecstasy.

This woman, who is the mother of her own
Invention yet seems driven by the storms
And seasons of nature's one design
Is humbled not by her own strength
But by the gentler souls she touches
Like a warm and fleeting breeze,
Then sleeps on the ground
Of her own ambition.

This woman, who is the child of past
Omissions and despair, lingered not
Where the soft winds of time could sooth
The grip of hurt or make it seem less hurting.
She is the quintessential child who
Loves the healing hand of caring
But losses herself beneath
A sky of compassion.

The woman, who is the goddess of
My own desires, has crept in
Slowly and silently to the dark room
Whose door I thought was bolted shut
And placed there the wreath of her own beauty,
The passion of her spirit is the
Passion of my own, the heart within
Her breast beats as my own.

MUSINGS

To the Irish, nothing is ever easy. Perhaps living with them is the most difficult of all. Everything is colored by the most recent joy or disaster; boundless love, bottomless despair. They are consumed by the sad happiness of cynicism. I am Irish.

-from a note to my wife upon the gift of the small book, "Irish Writers."

The School Bus

My first cup of coffee is poured and I sit and sip it each morning at the glass-top table in the sunroom as I watch the school bus turn onto my street a block away. It labors past my window as the faceless driver grinds the gears in shifting. The long yellow vehicle strikes me as oddly out of place on my broad street lined with neatly trimmed lawns on which slate-roofed houses stand silently in the unroused early morning.

A few rows behind the driver, perhaps halfway back, sits a single young student, about a six-grader, I guess. He is black, and faceless too. I wonder if he ponders, as I do, the school bus whose route takes it through a childless neighborhood.

It becomes my ritual as autumn slowly gives way to winter and the morning light comes later each day to have my coffee and wait with a little anticipation for the school bus to pass by with only the little black boy as passenger. I am somehow reassured by the sameness and the routine of seeing the bus and the boy sitting alone by the window in the dark interior.

On a Wednesday morning in early spring, I again am waiting with coffee for the bus. I see it turn the corner, the driver at the wheel, the bus struggling for speed. It passes by my window and I see only the driver; there are no passengers. Where is the boy, I asked myself with a slight smile. Out with a cold or maybe the flu; it's going around I hear.

The bus still comes by my window each weekday morning as I sip hot coffee at my glass-top table. But now it is always empty save for the driver. I miss seeing the nameless little black boy, I wish I could see his young face again.

Uncle Edward

When he came home from the war he did not say much, and he said nothing about the war itself. He had been wounded. His knee had been replaced with some kind of metal or composite parts that seemed to work pretty well; he said it ached when it rained. It was his right knee and he walked with a slight but noticeable limp although he never used a cane.

It was only with my father, his brother, that he seemed at ease. I would see them, and watch them in the back yard from the kitchen window early in the evening, sitting on the old painted steel glider under the pecan tree. Sometimes it seemed like hours. Uncle Edward would roll one cigarette after another and my dad puffed his pipe, constantly relighting it. But when I think about it, there was more silence between them than conversation. There were long periods of time when neither man appeared to speak, my uncle gazing at the cigarette in his hand, lost in another world, and my father just content with the silence and what was passing between them.

After the surgery and a stay hospital in Hawaii, my uncle came to stay with us. His wife had taken up with a traveling evangelist while he was gone to war and had moved on with him. I think there may have been a child involved, but I never knew if it was Uncle Edward's or the preacher's. Like many things in my family, it was never openly discussed. But it was exciting having him in our home.

Sometimes my two best friends, Junior and John David, came over and we camped out in a pup tent in the back yard. Uncle Edward would come round just before dark to check on us. He said he wanted to see if we were "squared away" and if the area was "secure". We did not know exactly what these terms meant, but we knew that it was military lingo coming from someone who had been in a real, far away war. We imagined what it felt like to be men. We imagined that we might someday be heroes too. Heroes like my Uncle Edward.

The boy went to see the old man again for some reason, though they had hardly ever spoken He waited out on the porch, alone, staring out across the brown marsh, thinking about fishing the creek today, when the tide was right.

"Come on in, boy."

The porch boards creaked and gave as he walked to the screen door and quietly opened it. The body, long and thin, lay in the large feather bed where lives were begun and where they ended too. As consistent as the tides. It was as if the old man was sleeping, deep and restful, after a long hot day in the field cutting and turning the sandy soil.

"He ain't much to look now. Never was," she said, holding back a sob.

"He looks all right to me," returned the boy.

He was still the same man, black and old, but he was not bent anymore or tired. All the things that had gone before were in his face, etched there indelibly; sad stories, sadder lives, and things shattered. Now, peace.

An early morning wind, wet and smelling of salt and oysters, rustled the thin dingy curtains, and seemed to blend naturally with the woman's gentle weeping. The cotton in the patch out behind the shack swayed gently in the breeze too.

They just stood there. Then he noticed the sun was up good now, white and hot. He touched the edge of the low bed and turned back toward the door, and left the room with the woman standing there looking down.

Yes, he would fish the creek today.

www.ingramcontent.com/pod-product-compliance
Lightning Source LLC
Chambersburg PA
CBHW010357310726
48979CB00006B/1069

* 9 7 8 0 9 9 8 1 0 7 1 9 6 *